# Pinkalicious

WRITTEN BY
Victoria Kann &
Elizabeth Kann

ILLUSTRATED BY
Victoria Kann

HarperCollins Publishers

It was a rainy day, too wet to go outside.
Mummy said, "Let's make cupcakes!
What colour do you want?"
"Pink!" I said. "Pink, pink, *pink*!"

Mummy put in some pink.
"More!" I cried. "More, more, more!"

I gobbled up a couple of cupcakes while Mummy and I frosted them. They were so yummy—they were PINKALICIOUS! I offered one to Peter, my little brother, but he is very picky and didn't want to eat his. So I ate it.

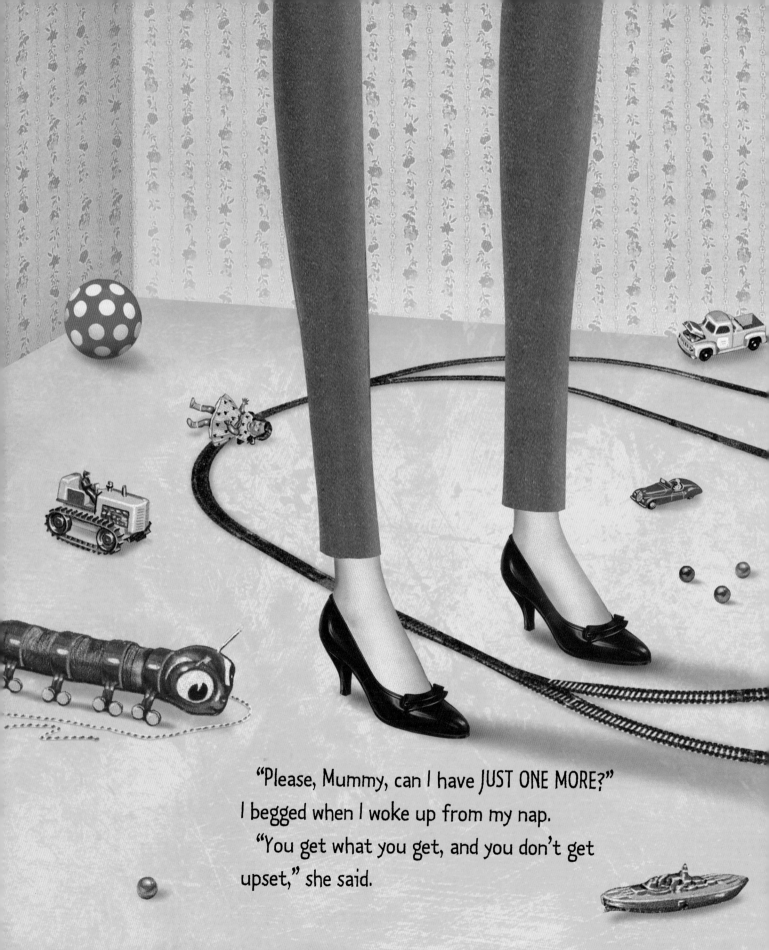

"Please, Mummy, can I have JUST ONE MORE?"
I begged when I woke up from my nap.
   "You get what you get, and you don't get
upset," she said.

But I got very upset.

After dinner I ate more cupcakes.
Then I refused to go to bed.
"Just one more pink cupcake, and
I'll go to sleep," I promised.

Daddy waved a tired finger at me. "You have had ENOUGH!"

The next morning when I woke up, I was PINK! My face was pink, my hands were pink, and my belly was the colour of a sunset.

Daddy thought I had played with
markers, so he gave me a bath.
The pink did not come off.

My hair was the colour of raspberry sorbet. I cried because I was so beautiful. I even had PINK tears. I put on my pink fairy princess dress and twirled in front of the mirror, while Mummy speed-dialed the paediatrician.

"I'm Pinkerbelle! Look at me, I'm Pinkerbelle!" I sang.

Mummy grabbed her purse.

"Just one more cupcake! PLEASE JUST ONE MORE!" I yelled on the way out the door. Mummy took me right to the doctor's office.

Dr. Wink looked at me and said, "You have a very rare and acute case of Pinkititis."

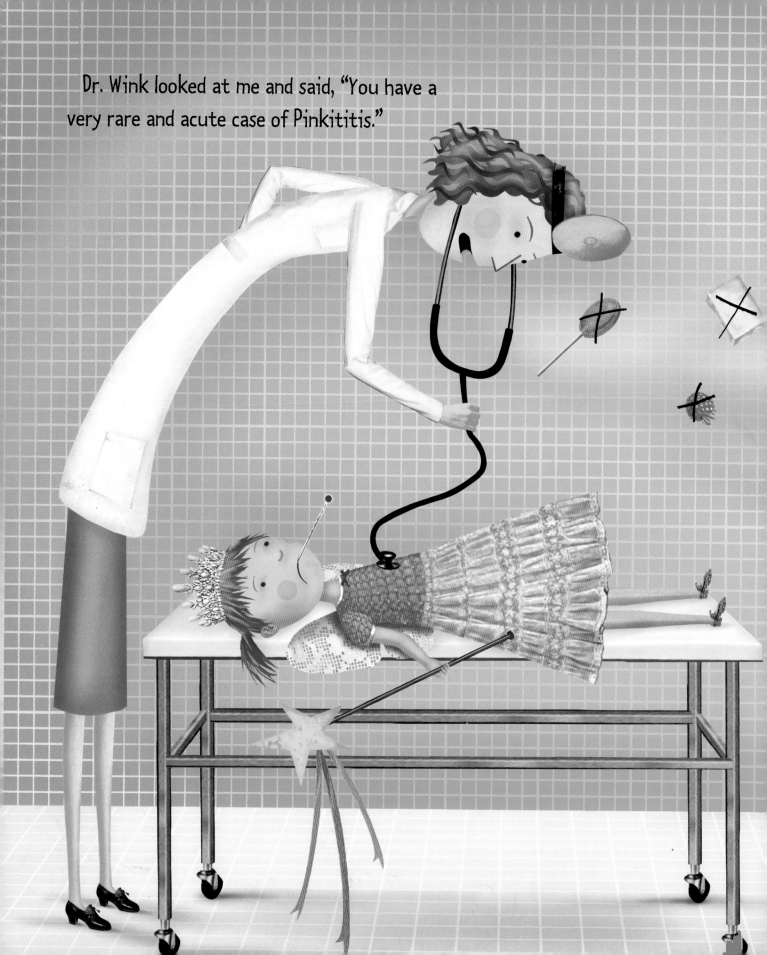

I guess that's not the worst thing that could happen.

Just call me PINKERELLA!

Then Dr. Wink said, "For the next week, no more pink cupcakes, pink bubble gum, or pink cotton candy." (BOO!)

"To return to normal, you must eat a steady diet of green food." (YUCK!)

On the way home, we stopped at the park.
My friend Alison was there, but she didn't see me
because I blended in with the pink peonies.
When I waved to Alison, a bumblebee landed on my nose.
"Buzz off! I am not a flower!" I scolded the bee.

Soon I was surrounded by bees, butterflies, and birds.
"MUMMY," I cried, "please take me home!"

When we left the park, I asked Mummy
if I could eat another pink cupcake when
we got home.

"Don't you remember what the doctor
told you?" she said. "NO MORE CUPCAKES!"

Peter tugged at my pinktails. "I wish I
were pink like you," he said.

He was green with envy.

That night, I pretended to eat my dinner of mushy, dark green vegetables. After everyone went to sleep, I sneaked into the kitchen, climbed onto a chair, and reached on my tippy toes to the top of the refrigerator, where Mummy had hidden the cupcakes.

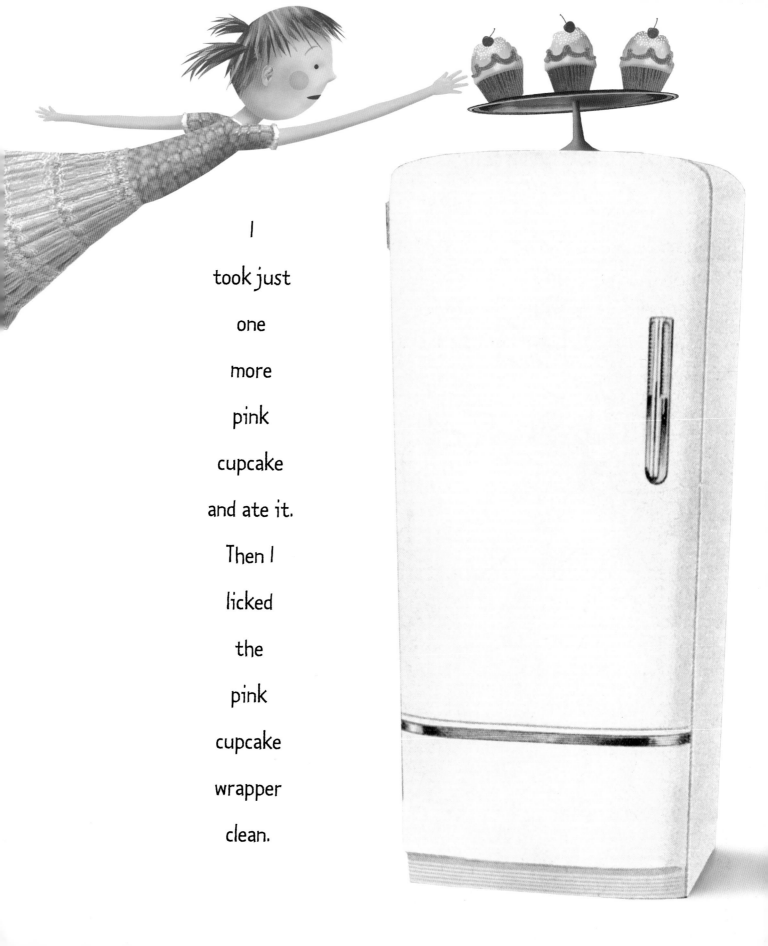

I
took just
one
more
pink
cupcake
and ate it.
Then I
licked
the
pink
cupcake
wrapper
clean.

When I woke up in the morning,
I felt different. I ran to the mirror
and peered at my reflection.

I was a deeper pink than I had ever
seen. In fact, I was no longer pink.

I was red!

"Oh, no, not RED!" I screamed.
I didn't want to be red. I should NOT
have eaten that pink cupcake last
night! I wanted to be myself again.
I knew what I had to do.

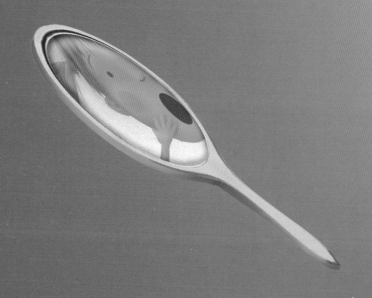

I opened the fridge, held my nose, and squeezed a bottle of icky green relish onto my tongue. I ate pickles and spinach, olives and okra. I choked down artichokes, gagged on grapes, and burped up Brussels sprouts. Next thing I knew, my arms tickled, my ears tingled, and my feet twitched.

Green Tea

RELISH

SUGAR PEAS
HONEY POD

I was no longer red. I was no longer
pink. I was me, and I was beautiful.
"So what happened to the rest of the
cupcakes, Pinkalicious?" Daddy asked.
Just then Peter ran in and yelled . . .

"Pink-a-boo!"

To Jaison and Ashley
—E.K.

To Christina and Leigha
—V.K.

And to our parents, Patricia and Steve,
with a special thank-you to Jill.

Cupcakes for all!

Pinkalicious
Text copyright © 2006 by Elizabeth Kann and Victoria Kann
Illustrations copyright © 2006 by Victoria Kann

Printed in China

Library of Congress Cataloging-in-Publication Data is available.
ISBN-10: 0-06-194447-5
ISBN-13: 978-0-06-194447-5

Typography by Stephanie Bart-Horvath
1 2 3 4 5 6 7 8 9 10
❖
First Edition